W9-BUB-910

FOR MY FATHER AND GRANDFATHER,
WHO SHOWED ME THAT COMEDY CAN
CONQUER CRANKY, EVERY TIME.
-SB

FOR MY PARENTS,
WHO PUT UP WITH MY CRANKINESS.
-DS

ABOUT THIS BOOK

EVERY MORNING DURING THE ENTIRE PRODUCTION OF THIS BOOK, DAN SANTAT WOULD MAKE HIMSELF GOOD AND CRANKY BY DEPRIVING HIMSELF OF COFFEE. HAVING JUST THE RIGHT AMOUNT OF CRANKINESS WAS IMPERATIVE TO THIS PROJECT. HE ILLUSTRATED THE BOOK USING ADOBE PHOTOSHOP, EVEN THOUGH HIS COMPUTER CRASHED ALL THE TIME. DAN THEN DECIDED TO HAND-LETTER EVERY SINGLE WORD, NOT REALIZING THERE WERE A *LOT* OF WORDS IN THIS BOOK.

CRANKENSTEIN IS THE EMBODIMENT OF DAN SANTAT'S PURE RAGE.

... AND HE DID IT ALL FOR YOU.

THE FOLLOWING MONSTERS CONTRIBUTED TO THE MAKING OF THIS BOOK

EDITOR: CONNIE "NOSFERATHSU" HSU
ART DIRECTOR AND DESIGNER: DAVE "CHUPACAPLAN" CAPLAN
PRODUCTION MANAGER: CHARLOTTE "TRANSYLVEANEYIA" VEANEY
PRODUCTION EDITOR: MARTHA "CIPOLDEMORT" CIPOLLA

LITTLE, BROWN AND COMPANY • HACHETTE BOOK GROUP
237 PARK AVENUE, NEW YORK, NY 10017
VISIT OUR WEBSITE AT WWW.LB-KIDS.COM

LITTLE, BROWN AND COMPANY IS A DIVISION OF HACHETTE BOOK GROUP, INC.
THE LITTLE, BROWN NAME AND LOGO ARE TRADEMARKS OF HACHETTE BOOK GROUP, INC.

FIRST EDITION: AUGUST 2013

LIBRARY OF CONGRESS CATALOGING-IN-PUBLICATION DATA

BERGER, SAMANTHA.
CRANKENSTEIN / BY SAMANTHA BERGER; ILLUSTRATED BY DAN SANTAT.—1ST ED. P. CM.
SUMMARY: A BOY WHO LOOKS ORDINARY TRANSFORMS INTO GRUMBLING CRANKENSTEIN WHEN FACED WITH A RAINY DAY, A MELTING POPSICLE, OR BEDTIME, BUT EVERYTHING CHANGES WHEN HE MEETS A FELLOW CRANKENSTEIN.
ISBN 978-0-316-12656-4 [1. BEHAVIOR—FICTION.] I. SANTAT, DAN, ILL. II. TITLE.
PZ7.B452136Cr 2013 • [E]—dc23 • 2012029480

10 9 8 7 6 5 4 3 2 1

SC

PRINTED IN CHINA

CRANKENSTEIN

WRITTEN by
SAMANTHA BERGER

ILLUSTRATED by
DAN SANTAT

LITTLE, BROWN AND COMPANY
NEW YORK BOSTON

6:59
HAVE YOU SEEN CRANKENSTEIN?

OH, YOU WOULD *TOTALLY* KNOW IF YOU HAD.

YOU WOULD SAY,

GOOD MORNING!!
HOW ARE YOU?

CRANKENSTEIN WOULD SAY,

MEHHRRRRR!

YOU WOULD SAY,

WHO WANTS PANCAKES?

EMPTY ↑

SYRUP →

CRANKENSTEIN WOULD SAY,

MEHHRRRR!!

YOU WOULD SAY,

TIME FOR

SCHOOL!

CRANKENSTEIN WOULD SAY,
MEHHRRRR!!!

YOU MIGHT SEE CRANKENSTEIN
WHEN IT'S SUPER RAINY OUTSIDE...

OR WHEN IT'S EXTRA COLD ON HALLOWEEN...

OR WHEN IT'S **WAY** TOO HOT FOR POPSICLES.

ESPECIALLY WHEN IT'S WAY TOO HOT FOR POPSICLES.

YOU CAN BE SURE TO FIND CRANKENSTEIN IN A LONG, LONG LINE.

CRANKENSTEIN *HATES* LONG, LONG LINES.

OR WHEN IT'S TIME TO TAKE
GROSS COUGH SYRUP.
DR. GIGGLES
COUGH
SYRUP

CRANKENSTEIN *HATES*
GROSS COUGH SYRUP.

AND YOU'LL *DEFINITELY* SEE CRANKENSTEIN
WHEN YOU SAY IT'S BEDTIME.

CRANKENSTEIN *HATES* WHEN YOU SAY IT'S BEDTIME.

MEHRRRR!

YES, THAT CRANKENSTEIN IS SOME PRETTY SCARY BUSINESS, ALL RIGHT.

BUT JUST WHEN YOU THINK THAT MONSTER IS HERE TO STAY...

MEHHRRRRR!

HE MIGHT DO SOMETHING
THAT SURPRISES YOU.
BECAUSE WHEN CRANKENSTEIN
MEETS *ANOTHER* CRANKENSTEIN...

IT JUST MIGHT MAKE HIM...

LAUGH.

AHAHAHA
AHAHAHA
HAHAHA
HAHAHAH

...AT LEAST FOR NOW.

BECAUSE THAT CRANKENSTEIN?

...BUT DEFINITELY NOT TODAY.